D0558136

2⁵⁰

Esprit de Corps

By the same author

*

ESPRIT DE CORPS

Sketches from Diplomatic Life

by

Lawrence Durrell

Illustrated by

V. H. DRUMMOND

FABER AND FABER

London · Boston

First published in 1957
by Faber and Faber Limited
3 Queen Square London WC1
First published in this edition 1961
Reprinted 1963, 1966, 1969, 1972, 1976 and 1979
Printed in Great Britain by
Whitstable Litho Ltd Whitstable Kent
All rights reserved

ISBN 0 571 05667 9

© *Lawrence George Durrell*
1957

Contents

The Ghost Train

I like Antrobus. I can't really say why—I think it is because he takes everything so frightfully seriously. He is portentous—always dropping into a whisper, clicking his tongue, making a po-face, pursing his lips, turning the palms of his hand outwards and making "what-would-you" gestures.

We've served together in a number of foreign capitals, he as a regular of the career, I as a contract officer: which explains why he is now a heavily padded senior in Southern while I am an impoverished writer. Nevertheless, whenever I'm in London he gives me lunch at his club and we talk about the past—those happy days passed in foreign capitals "lying abroad" for our country.

"The Ghost Train episode", said Antrobus, "was a bit before your time. I only mention it because I can think of nothing which illustrates the peculiar hazards of Diplomatic Life so well. In fact it throws them into Stark Relief.

"Every nation has its particular *idée fixe*. For the Yugoslavs it is trains. Nothing can compare for breathtaking romance with the railway train. Railway engines have to be put under armed guard when not in motion or they would be poked to pieces by the enquiring peasantry. No other object arouses the concupiscence of the Serb like a train. They drool over it, old boy, positively drool. *Ils bavent*.

"You twig this the minute you alight from the Orient Express at Belgrade because there is something queer about the station building itself. It leans to one side. It is neatly cracked from platform level to clock-tower. Moreover there are several distinct sets of ruts in the concrete of the platform which are highly suggestive. The first porter you engage will clear up the mystery. Apparently every fifteenth train or so leaps the buffers, grinds across the Freight Section and buries itself in the booking office. No one is ever hurt and the whole town joyfully bands together to dig the engine out. Everyone is rather proud of this particular idiosyncrasy. It is part of the Serbian way of life.

"Well, being aware of this as I was, I could not help being a bit concerned when Nimic in the Protocol hinted that the Diplomatic Corps was to be sent to Zagreb for Liberation Day in a special train which would prove once and for all that the much-vaunted Yugoslav heavy industry was capable of producing machinery every bit as good as the degenerate Capitalist West. This tip was accompanied by dark looks and winks and all efforts to probe the mystery further proved vain. A veil of secrecy (one of the seven veils of Communist diplomacy) was drawn over the subject. Naturally we in the Corps were interested, while those who had served for some time in the Balkans were perturbed. '*Mon Dieu*,' said Du Bellay the

French Minister gravely, '*si ces animaux veulent jouer aux locos avec le Corps Diplomatique . . .*' He was voicing the Unspoken Thoughts of many of us.

"There was no further information forthcoming about the Ghost Train as we jokingly called it, so we sat back and waited for Liberation Day. Sure enough the customary fat white envelope appeared ten days before from the Protocol. I opened mine with a troubled curiosity. It announced that the Corps would be travelling by a Special Train which would be placed at its disposal. The train itself was called 'The Liberation-Celebration Machine'.

"Even Polk-Mowbray looked a bit grave. 'What sort of Devil-Car do you think it will be?' he said apprehensively. I couldn't enlighten him, alas. 'It's probably a chain-drive Trojan with some carriages built around it in plywood.'

"There was a short-lived movement among the Corps to go by road instead and thus sidestep the 'Liberation-Celebration Machine' but the Doyen put his foot down. Such a defection would constitute a grave slight. The Yugoslav heavy industry would be hurt by our refusal to allow it to unveil the marvels of modern science to us. Reluctantly we all accepted. 'Butch' Benbow, the naval attaché, who was clairvoyant and who dabbled in astrology, took the omens. Apparently they were not propitious. 'All I can see is clouds of smoke,' he said hoarsely, looking up from the progressed chart on his desk. 'And someone gets a severe scalp wound—probably you, sir.'

"Polk-Mowbray started. 'Now, look here,' he said, 'let's have no alarm and despondency on this one. If the Yugoslav heavy industry gives me even a trifling scalp wound I'll see that there is an International Incident over it.'

"The day drew inexorably nearer. The Special Train, we learned, was to be met in a siding just outside Belgrade. There is a small station there, the name of which I forget. Here at the appointed time, which was dusk, we duly presented ourselves in full *tenue*. There were to be flowers and speeches by representatives of the Yugoslav Heavy Industry. Most of the representatives looked nearly as heavy as their industry. But I couldn't take my eyes off the train.

"I'm not saying it was gaudy. It was absolutely breathtaking. The three long coaches were made of painted and carved timber; flowers, birds, liberation heroes, *cachesexes*, emblematic devices, post-horns—everything you can imagine, all carved and painted according to the peasant fancy. The general effect was that of a Sicilian market-cart with painted and carved side-boards—or the poop of some seventeenth-century galleon. Every blacksmith, wheelwright and cartwright in Serbia must have had a hand in it. *'C'est un chalet Tyroléan ou quoi?'* I heard Du Bellay say under his breath. His scepticism was shared by us all.

"We entered and found our reserved carriages which seemed normal enough. The band played. We accepted a wreath or two. Then we set off in the darkness to the braying of donkeys and cocks and the rasping of trombones. We were off across the rolling Serbian plains.

"Two things were immediately obvious. All this elaborate woodwork squeaked and groaned calamitously, ear-splittingly. How were we to get any sleep? But more serious still was the angle of inclination of the second coach with the Heads of Mission in it. It was about thirty

degrees out of centre and was only, it seemed, held upright by the one immediately before and behind it. It was
clear that the Yugoslav heavy industry had mislaid its
spirit-level while it was under construction. People who
looked out of the windows on one side had the illusion
that the ground was coming up to hit them. I paid Polk-
Mowbray a visit to see if he was all right and found him
looking rather pale, and drawn up on the higher elevation
of the coach like someone on a sinking ship. The noise
was so great that we couldn't speak—we had to shout:
'My God,' I heard him cry out, 'what is to become of us
all?' It was a little difficult to say. We were now gathering
speed. The engine was a very old one. It had been
abandoned before the war by an American film company
and the Yugoslavs had tied it together with wire. Its
gaping furnace, which was white hot, was being passion-
ately fed by some very hairy men in cloth caps who
looked like Dostoevsky's publishers. It seemed to me
that the situation had never looked graver. Despite its
age, however, it had managed to whip up a good forty-
five. And every five hundred yards it would groan and
void a bucketful of white clinker into the night which
set fire to the grass on either side of the track. From far
off we must have looked like an approaching forest fire.

"Another feature of the 'Liberation-Celebration
Machine' was an ingenious form of central heating which
could not be turned off, and as none of the windows
opened, the temperature inside the coaches rapidly
mounted into the hundreds. People were fanning themselves with their tall hats. Old man, never have I seen the
Corps subjected to such a strain. Sleep was impossible.
The lights would not turn off. The wash basins appeared
to empty into each other. And all the time we had the

ghastly thought of all the Heads of Mission in the Hanging Coach, drinking brandy and gibbering with fright as we sped onwards through the night.

"The chance of some frightful accident taking place was far from remote and consequently nobody was able to relax. We did not even dare to get into pyjamas but sat about in that infernal racket staring desperately at one another and starting at every regurgitation of the engine, every shiver and squeak of the coaches. The American Ambassador was so overcome that he spent the night singing 'Nearer My God To Thee'. Some said that he had had the forethought to take a case of rye into his compartment with him. Madame Fawzia, the Egyptian Ambassadress, spent the night on the floor of her compartment deep in prayer. I simply did not dare to think of Polk-Mowbray. From time to time when the wind changed the whole train was enveloped in a cloud of rich dense smoke containing fragments of half-digested coal the size of hailstones. But still the ghoulish crew in the engine-cab plied their grisly shovels and on we sped with mournful shrieks and belches.

"At two in the morning there was a ghastly rending noise as we entered the station of Slopsy Blob, named after the famous Independence fighter. The Hanging Coach somehow got itself engaged with the tin dado which ran along the roof of the station and ripped it off as clean as a whistle, by the same token almost decapitating one of the drivers. The noise was appalling and the whole Corps let out a unified shriek of terror. I have never heard diplomats scream like that before or since—and I never want to. A lot of cherubs and floral devices were ripped off the Hanging Coach in the encounter and the people in the rear coaches found themselves assailed by a hail of coloured fragments of wood which made them shriek the louder. It was all over in a moment.

"Then we were out in the night once more racing across the dark plain, the brothers Karamazov still plying the engine with might and main. It is possible that, in the manner of Serbs, they had heard nothing. We spent the rest of the night in Sleepless Vigil, old man. The guardian angel of the Yugoslav Heavy Industry must have been with us for nothing much worse happened. But it was a pretty dispirited and shaken dip corps that was finally dragged into Zagreb station on that Liberation morning. I can tell you, never was liberation so much in the forefront of everyone's thoughts.

"It must have been about six o'clock when we stormed into Zagreb squealing and blowing out an Etna of steam. The brakes had been applied some three miles outside the station and their ear-splitting racket had to be heard to be believed.

"But this was not the end. Though we missed the red carpet by a quarter of a mile, and though the waiting dignitaries and the Zagreb Traction and Haulage Workers' Band padded down the platform after us our troubles were not yet at an end. It was found that the doors of the coaches on the platform side were fast shut and could not be opened. I suppose Zagreb Station must have been on the opposite side of the track from Belgrade Station and consequently nobody dreamed that we should need more than one exit from the train. It was, of course, fearfully humiliating. We leaned against the windows making inarticulate gestures of goodwill and vague grimaces in the direction of the Traction Haulage Workers' Band and the Liberation Reception Committee.

"We must have looked like a colony of dispossessed fairground apes pining for the old life of the trees. After a good deal of mopping and mowing there was nothing for it but to climb out of the Zagreb Flyer on to the permanent way and walk round the train to the reception point. This we somewhat shamefacedly did. But when all was said and done it was good to feel terra firma under our feet once more. Drawn up in order of precedence on Zagreb platform we submitted to the Liberation anthem sung by the Partisan choir in a register so low that it could not drown the merry cries of self-congratulation with which the Karamazov brothers were greeting the morn. Their observations were punctuated by blasts of hot steam and whiffs of sound from the whistle of the Liberation-Celebration Machine which looked even more improbable in the cold morning light than it had done the evening before.

"All this went off as well as such things can be expected to do; but sleepy as we were a sudden chill struck our hearts at a phrase in the Speech of Welcome which plainly indicated that the authorities were expecting us to make the return journey in the Liberation-Celebration Machine on the following day. This gave us all food for thought. Madame Fawzia made an involuntary retching noise which was interpreted by our hosts as an expression of joy. Several other ladies in the Corps showed a disposition to succumb to the vapours at this piece of intelligence. But the old training dies hard. There was many a tight lip and beady eye but not a word was said until we were assembled for breakfast in the card room of the Slopsy Blob Hotel. Then the pent-up floodwaters of emotion overflowed. Ambassadors, Ministers, Secretaries of Embassy and their wives began as one man to gesticulate and gabble. It was a moving scene. Some called upon the Gods to witness that they would never travel by train again; others spoke wonderingly of the night they had just spent when the whole of their past life flashed before them as if on a screen; the wife of the Spanish Republican Minister, by far the most deeply shaken by events, fell upon the Doyen, the Polish Ambassador, and named him as responsible before God for our safety and well-being. It was an interesting study in national types. The Egyptians screamed, the Finns and Norwegians snarled, the Slav belt pulled at each other's lapels as if they were milking goats. The Greeks made Promethean gestures at everyone. (They could afford to take the Balanced View since they had already hired the only six taxis in Zagreb and were offering seats for the return journey at a thousand dinars each.)

"One thing emerged clearly from all this. The Corps was in a state of open mutiny and would not easily be persuaded to entrain once more with the Brothers Karamazov. The Doyen pleaded in vain. We struck various national attitudes all round the room. The Italian Ambassadress who looked as if her anger would succeed in volatilizing her went so far as to draw up her dress and show the company a bruise inflicted on her during the journey. As for Polk-Mowbray, he did indeed have a scalp wound—an egg-shaped protuberance on the crown of his head where he had doubtless been struck by a passing railway station. It was clear that the journey had aged him.

"Well, that day most of us spent the time in bed with cold compresses and aspirin. In the evening we attended a performance of the Ballet and a Torchlight Tattoo. Liberation Day was at an end. That night the Doyen convened another meeting in the hotel at which he harangued us about diplomatic procedure in general and our obligations to the Service in particular. In vain. We were determined not to travel back on the Ghost Train. He pleaded with us but we were adamant. That evening a flock of telegrams fluttered into the Protocol Department of the Ministry of Foreign Affairs—telegrams pleading sudden illness, pressure of work, unforeseen political developments, migraine, influenza, neuritis or Events Beyond the Writer's Control. At dawn a convoy of taxis set out on the homeward track bearing the shattered remnants of the Corps, unshaven, unhonoured, but still alive, still breathing. . . . In a way I was sorry for the Brothers Karamazov and the Liberation-Celebration Machine. God knows, one did not wish them ill. But I must confess I was not surprised to read in the paper a week later that this latest triumph of the Yugoslav Heavy Industry had jumped the points at Slopsy Blob and finished the good work it had begun by carrying away most of the station buildings. No one was hurt. No one ever is in Serbia. Just badly shaken and frightened out of one's wits. It is all, when you come to think of it, part of the Serbian Way of Life. . . ."

2

Case History

Last week, Polk-Mowbray's name came up again—we had read of his retirement that morning, in *The Times*. We had both served under him in Madrid and Moscow, while Antrobus himself had been on several missions headed by him—Sir Claud Polk-Mowbray, O.M., K.C.M.G., and all that sort of thing.

Talking of him, Antrobus did his usual set of facial jerks culminating in an expression like a leaky flowerpot, and said: "You know, old man, thinking of Polk-Mowbray today and all the different places we've served, I suddenly thought 'My God, in Polk-Mowbray we have witnessed the gradual destruction of an Ambassador's soul'."

I was startled by this observation.

"I mean," went on Antrobus, "that gradually, insidiously, the Americans got him."

"How do you mean, 'the Americans got him'?"

Antrobus clicked his tongue and lofted his gaze.

"Perhaps you didn't know, perhaps you were not a Silent Witness as I was."

"I don't honestly think I was."

"Do you remember Athens '37, when I was first secretary?"

"Of course."

"Polk-Mowbray was a perfectly normal well-balanced Englishman then. He had all the fashionable weaknesses of the eighteenth-century gentleman. He fenced, he played the recorder."

"I remember all that."

"But something else too. Think back."

"I'm thinking. . . ."

Antrobus leaned forward and said with portentous triumph: "He wrote good English in those days." Then he sat back and stared impressively at me down the long bony incline of his nose. He allowed the idea to soak in.

Of course what he meant by good English was the vaguely orotund and ornamental eighteenth-century stuff which was then so much in vogue. A sort of mental copperplate prose.

"I remember now," I said, "committing the terrible sin of using the phrase 'the present set-up' in a draft despatch on economics." (It came back gashed right through with the scarlet pencil which only Governors and Ambassadors are allowed to wield—and with something nasty written in the margin.)

"Ah," said Antrobus, "so you remember that. What did he write?"

" 'The thought that members of my staff are beginning to introject American forms into the Mother Tongue has given me great pain. I am ordering Head of Chancery to instruct staff that no despatches to the Foreign Secretary should contain phrases of this nature.' "

"Phew."

"As you say—phew."

"But Nemesis", said Antrobus, "was lying in wait for him, old chap. Mind you," he added in the sort of tone which always sounds massively hypocritical to foreigners simply because it is, "mind you I'm not anti-American myself—never was, never will be. And there were some things about the old Foreign Office Prose Style—the early Nicolson type."

"It was practically Middle English."

"No, what I objected to was the Latin tag. Polk-Mowbray was always working one in. If possible he liked to slip one in at the beginning of a despatch. '*Hominibus plenum, amicis vacuum* as Cato says', he would kick off. The damnable thing was that at times he would forget whether it was Cato who said it. I was supposed to know, as Head of Chancery. But I never did. My classics have always been fluffy. I used to flash to my Pears Encyclopedia or my Brewer, swearing all the time."

"He sacked young Pollit for attributing a remark in Tacitus to Suetonius."

"Yes. It was very alarming. I'm glad those days are over."

"But Nemesis. What form did he take?"

"She, old man. *She*. Nemesis is always a woman. Polk-Mowbray was sent on a brief mission to the States in the middle of the war."

"Ah."

"He saw her leading a parade wrapped in the Stars and Stripes and twirling a baton. Her name was Carrie Potts. She was what is known as a majorette. I know. Don't wince. No, he didn't marry her. But she was a Milestone, old fellow. From then on the change came about, very gradually, very insidiously. I noticed that he dropped the Latin tag in his drafts. Then he began to leave the 'u' out of words like 'colour' and 'valour'. Finally, and this is highly significant, he sent out a staff circular saying that any of the secretaries caught using phrases like *quid pro quo*, *sine qua non*, *ad hoc*, *ab initio*, *ab ovo* and *status quo* would be transferred. This was a bombshell. We were deprived at a blow of practically our whole official vocabulary. Moreover as he read through the circular I distinctly heard him say under his breath: 'This will pin their ears back.' You can imagine, old fellow, I was stiff with horror. Of course, the poor fellow is not entirely to blame; he was fighting the disease gamely enough. It was just too much for him. I found a novel by Damon Runyon in his desk-drawer one day. I admit that he had the good taste to blush when he saw I'd found it. But by this time he had begun to suffer from dreadful slips of the tongue. At a cocktail party for instance he referred to me as his 'sidekick'. I was too polite to protest but I must admit it rankled. But there was a much more serious aspect to the business. His despatches began to take a marked transpontine turn. By God, you'll never believe it but I kept coming across expressions like 'set-up', 'frame-up', 'come-back', and even 'gimmick'. I ask you—*gimmick*." Antrobus blew out his breath in a cloud of horror. "As you can imagine," he went on after a pause, "the F.O. was troubled by the change in his reporting. Worst of all, other Ministers and Ambassadors junior to him and easily influenced showed some disposition to copy this sort of thing. Finally it got to such a pitch that all despatches before being printed in Intel-summary form had to pass through a sieve: they established an office in the Rehabilitation section specially for deformed English. Then you remember the Commission on Official English and the book called *Foreign Office Prose—How to Write It?*"

"Yes. One of the worst written books I've ever read."

"Well, be that as it may, it was the direct outcome of Polk-Mowbray's activities. It was a last desperate attempt to stop the rot, old man. It was too late, of course, because by this time that dreadful Churchill chap was wandering all over the globe in a siren suit waving a Juliet at everyone. I need hardly add that Mowbray himself ordered a siren suit which he referred to as his 'sneakers'. He used to potter round the Embassy grounds in them— a bit furtively, of course, but nevertheless . . . there it was." Antrobus paused for a long moment as he sorted out these painful memories. Then he said grimly, under his breath, and with dark contempt: "Faucet, elevator, phoney. I *ask* you."

"Yes," I said.

"Hatchet-man . . . disc-jockey . . . torch-singer."

"Yes. Yes. I follow you."

"I was terribly sad. Poor Polk-Mowbray. Do you know that he went to a Rotary meeting in a hand-painted tie depicting a nude blonde and referred to it in his speech as 'pulchritudinous'?"

"Never."

"He did." Antrobus nodded vigorously several times and took a savage swig at his drink. "He absolutely did."

"I suppose", I said after a moment, "that now he is retiring he will settle over there and integrate himself."

"He was offered a chance to go to Lake Success as a specialist on Global Imponderables, but he turned it down. Said the I.Q. wasn't high enough—whatever that meant. No, it's even more tragic. He has taken a villa outside Rome and intends to summer in Italy. I saw him

last week when I came back from the Athens Conference."

"You saw him?"

"Yes." Antrobus fell into a heavy brooding silence, evidently stirred to the quick. "I don't really know if I should tell you this," he said in a voice with a suspicion of choking in it. "It's such a nightmare."

"I won't repeat it."

"No. Please don't."

"I won't."

He gazed sadly at me as he signed his bar slips, waiting in true Foreign Office style until the servant was out of earshot. Then he leaned forward and said: "I ran into him near the *Fontana*, sitting in a little *trattoria*. He was dressed in check plus-fours with a green bush jacket and a cap with a peak. He was addressing a plate of spaghetti—and *do you know what*?"

"No. What?"

"There was a *Coca Cola* before him with a straw in it."

"Great heavens, Antrobus, you are jesting."

"My solemn oath, old man."

"It's the end."

"The very end. Poor Polk-Mowbray. I tried to cringe my way past him but he saw me and called out." Here Antrobus shuddered. "He said, quite distinctly, quite unequivocally, without a shadow of doubt—he said: '*Hiya!*' and made a sort of gesture in the air as of someone running his hand listlessly over the buttocks of a chorus girl. I won't imitate it in here, someone might see."

"I know the gesture you mean."

"Well," said Antrobus bitterly, "now you know the worst. I suppose it's a symptom of the age really." As we sauntered out of his club, acknowledging the porter's

26

greeting with a nod, he put on his soft black hat and put his umbrella into the crook of his arm. His face had taken on its graven image look—"a repository of the nation's darkest secrets". We walked in silence for a while until we reached my bus stop. Then he said: "Poor Polk-Mowbray. In Coca Cola veritas what?"

"Indeed," I said. There could not be a better epitaph.

Frying the Flag

"Of course, if there had been any justice in the world," said Antrobus, depressing his cheeks grimly. "If we ourselves had shown any degree of responsibility, the two old ladies would have been minced, would have been incinerated. Their ashes would have been trampled into some Serbian field or scattered in the sea off some Dalmatian island, like Drool or Snot. Or they would have been sold into slavery to the Bogomils. Or just simply crept up on from behind and murdered at their typewriters. I used to dream about it, old man."

"Instead of which they got a gong each."

"Yes. Polk-Mowbray put them up for an M.B.E. He had a perverted sense of humour. It's the only explanation."

"And yet time softens so many things. I confess I look back on the old *Central Balkan Herald* with something like nostalgia."

"Good heavens," said Antrobus, and blew out his cheeks. We were enjoying a stirrup-cup at his club before

28

taking a turn in the park. Our conversation, turning as it always did upon our common experiences abroad in the Foreign Service, had led us with a sort of ghastly inevitability to the sisters Grope; Bessie and Enid Grope, joint editor-proprietors of the *Central Balkan Herald* (circulation 500). They had spent all their lives in Serbia, for their father had once been Embassy chaplain and on retirement had elected to settle in the dusty Serbian plains. Where, however, they had inherited the old flat-bed press and the stock of battered Victorian faces, I cannot tell, but the fact remains that they had produced between them an extraordinary daily newspaper which remains without parallel in my mind after a comparison with newspapers in more than a dozen countries—"THE BALKAN HERALD KEEPS THE BRITISH FLAG FRYING"—that was the headline that greeted me on the morning of my first appearance in the Press Department. It was typical.

The reason for a marked disposition towards misprints was not far to seek; the composition room, where the paper was hand-set daily, was staffed by half a dozen hirsute Serbian peasants with greasy elf-locks and hands like shovels. Bowed and drooling and uttering weird eldritch-cries from time to time they went up and down the type-boxes with the air of half-emancipated baboons hunting for fleas. The master printer was called Icic (pronounced Itchitch) and he sat forlornly in one corner living up to his name by scratching himself from time to time. Owing to such laborious methods of composition the editors were hardly ever able to call for extra proofs; even as it was the struggle to get the paper out on the streets was grandiose to watch. Some time in the early thirties it had come out a day late and that day had never been made up. With admirable single-mindedness the sisters decided, so as not to leave gaps in their files, to keep the date twenty-four hours behind reality until such times as, by a superhuman effort, they could produce two newspapers in one day and thus catch up.

Bessie and Enid Grope sat in the editorial room which was known as the "den". They were both tabby in colouring and wore rusty black. They sat facing one another pecking at two ancient typewriters which looked as if they had been obtained from the Science Museum of the Victoria and Albert.

Bessie was News, Leaders, and Gossip; Enid was Features, Make-up and general Sub. Whenever they were at a loss for copy they would mercilessly pillage ancient copies of *Punch* or *Home Chat*. An occasional hole in the copy was filled with a ghoulish smudge—local block-making clearly indicated that somewhere a poker-work fanatic had gone quietly out of his mind. In this way the *Central Balkan Herald* was made up every morning and then delivered to the composition room where the chain-gang rapidly reduced it to gibberish. MINISTER FINED FOR KISSING IN PUBIC. WEDDING BULLS RING OUT FOR PRINCESS. QUEEN OF HOLLAND GIVES PANTY FOR EX-SERVICE MEN. MORE DOGS HAVE BABIES THIS SUMMER IN BELGRADE. BRITAINS NEW FLYING-GOAT.

In the thirties this did not matter so much but with the war and the growth of interest in propaganda both the Foreign Office and the British Council felt that an English newspaper was worth keeping alive in the Balkans if only to keep the flag flying. A modest subsidy and a free news service went a long way to help the sisters, though of course there was nothing to be done with the crew down in the composition room. "Mrs. Schwartkopf has cast off clothes of every description and invites

inspection", "In a last desperate spurt the Cambridge crew, urged on by their pox, overtook Oxford".

Every morning I could hear the whistles and groans and sighs as each of the secretaries unfolded his copy and addressed himself to his morning torture. On the floor above, Polk-Mowbray kept drawing his breath sharply at every misprint like someone who has run a splinter into his finger. At this time the editorial staff was increased by the addition of Mr. Tope, an elderly catarrhal man who made up the news page, thus leaving Bessie free to follow her bent in paragraphs on gardening ("How to Plant Wild Bubs") and other extravagances. It was understood that at some time in the remotest past Mr. Tope had been in love with Bessie but he "had never Spoken"; perhaps he had fallen in love with both sisters simultaneously and had been unable to decide which to marry. At all events he sat in the "den" busy with the world news; every morning he called on me for advice. "We want the *Herald* to play its full part in the war effort," he never failed to assure me gravely. "We are all in this together." There was little I could do for him.

At times I could not help feeling that the *Herald* was more trouble than it was worth. References, for example, to "Hitler's nauseating inversion—the rocket-bomb" brought an immediate visit of protest from Herr Schpünk the German *chargé*, dictionary in hand, while the early stages of the war were greeted with BRITAIN DROPS BIGGEST EVER BOOB ON BERLIN. This caused mild speculation as to whom this personage might be. Attempts, moreover, to provide serious and authoritative articles for the *Herald* written by members of the Embassy shared the same fate. Spalding, the commercial attaché who was trying to negotiate on behalf of the British

Mining Industry, wrote a painstaking survey of the wood resources of Serbia which appeared under the startling banner BRITAIN TO BUY SERBIAN TIT-PROPS, while the the military attaché who was rash enough to contribute a short strategic survey of Suez found that the phrase "Canal Zone" was printed without a "C" throughout. There was nothing one could do. "One feels so desperately ashamed," said Polk-Mowbray, "with all the resources of culture and so on that we have—that a British newspaper abroad should put out such disgusting gibberish. After all, it's semi-official, the Council has subsidized it specially to spread the British Way of Life. . . . It's not good enough."

But there was nothing much we could do. The *Herald* lurched from one extravagance to the next. Finally in the columns of Theatre Gossip there occurred a series of what Antrobus called Utter Disasters. The reader may be left to imagine what the Serbian compositors would be capable of doing to a witty urbane and deeply considered review of the 100,000th performance of *Charley's Aunt*.

The *Herald* expired with the invasion of Yugoslavia and the sisters were evacuated to Egypt where they performed prodigies of valour in nursing refugees. With the return to Belgrade, however, they found a suspicious Communist régime in power which ignored all their requests for permission to refloat the *Herald*. They brought their sorrows to the Embassy, where Polk-Mowbray received them with a stagey but absent-minded sympathy. He agreed to plead with Tito, but of course he never did. "If they start that paper up again," he told his Chancery darkly, "I shall resign." "They'd make a laughing stork out of you, sir," said Spalding. (The pre-war mission had been returned almost unchanged.)

Mr. Tope also returned and to everyone's surprise had Spoken and had been accepted by Bessie; he was now comparatively affluent and was holding the post which in the old days used to be known as Neuter's Correspondent—aptly or not who can say?

"Well, I think the issue was very well compounded by getting the old girls an M.B.E. each for distinguished services to the British Way of Life. I'll never forget the investiture with Bessie and Enid in tears and Mr. Tope swallowing like a toad. And all the headlines Spalding wrote for some future issue of the *Herald*: 'Sister Roasted in Punk Champage after solemn investitute'."

"It's all very well to laugh," said Antrobus severely, "but a whole generation of Serbs have had their English gouged and mauled by the *Herald*. Believe me, old man, only yesterday I had a letter from young Babic, you remember him?"

"Of course."

"For him England is peppered with fantastic placenames which he can only have got from the *Herald*. He says he enjoyed visiting Henleg Regatta and Wetminster Abbey; furthermore, he was present at the drooping of the colour; he further adds that the noise of Big Bun striking filled him with emotion; and that he saw a film about Florence Nightingale called 'The Lade With the Lump'. No, no, old man, say what you will the *Herald* has much to answer for. It is due to sinister influences like the Gropes and Topes of this world that the British Council's struggle is such an uphill one. Care for another?"

4

Jots and Tittles

"In Diplomacy," said Antrobus, "quite small things can be One's Undoing; things which in themselves may be Purely Inadvertent. The Seasoned Diplomat keeps a sharp eye out for these moments of Doom and does what he can to avert them. Sometimes he succeeds, but sometimes he fails utterly—and then Irreparable Harm ensues.

"Foreigners are apt to be preternaturally touchy in small ways and I remember important negotiations being spoilt sometimes by a slip of the tongue or an imagined slight. I remember an Italian personage, for example (let us call him the Minister for Howls and Smells), who with the temerity of ignorance swarmed up the wrong side of the C.-in-C. Med.'s Flagship in Naples harbour with a bunch of violets and a bottle of Strega as a gift from the Civil Servants of Naples. He was not only ordered off in rather stringent fashion but passes were made at him with a brass-shod boathook. This indignity cost us dear and we practically had to resort to massage to set things right.

"Then there was the Finnish Ambassador's wife in Paris who slimmed so rigorously that her stomach took to rumbling quite audibly at receptions. I suppose she was hungry. But no sooner did she walk into a room with a buffet in it than her stomach set up growls of protest. She tried to pass it off by staring hard at other people but it didn't work. Of course, people not in the know simply thought that someone upstairs was moving furniture about. But at private dinner parties this characteristic was impossible to disguise; she would sit rumbling at her guests who in a frenzy of politeness tried to raise their voices above the noise. She soon lost ground in the Corps. Silences would fall at her parties—the one thing that Diplomats fear more than anything else. When silences begin to fall, broken only by the rumblings of a lady's entrails, it is The Beginning of the End.

"But quite the most illuminating example of this sort of thing occurred on the evening when Polk-Mowbray swallowed a moth. I don't think I ever told you about it before. It is the sort of thing one only talks about in the strictest confidence. It was at a dinner party given to the Communist People's Serbian Trade and Timber Guild sometime during Christmas week back in '52. Yugoslavia at that time had just broken with Stalin and was beginning to feel that the West was not entirely populated by 'capitalist hyenas' as the press said. They were still wildly suspicious of us, of course, and it was a very hot and embarrassed little group of peasants dressed in dark suits who accepted Polk-Mowbray's invitation to dinner at the Embassy. Most of them spoke only their mother tongue. Comrade Bobok, however, the leader of the delegation, spoke a gnarled embryonic English. He was a huge sweating Bosnian peasant with a bald head. His number two, Pepic, spoke the sort of French that one imagines is learned in mission houses in Polynesia. From a diplomatist's point of view they were Heavy Going.

"I shall say nothing about their messy food habits; Drage the butler kept circling the table and staring at them as if he had gone out of his senses. We were all pretty sweaty and constrained by the time the soup plates were removed. The conversation was early cave-man stuff consisting of growls and snarls and weird flourishes of knife and fork. Bobok and Pepic sat on Polk-Mowbray's right and left respectively; they were flanked by Spalding the Commercial Attaché and myself. We were absolutely determined to make the evening a success. De Mandeville for some curious reason best known to himself had decreed that we should eat turkey with mustard and follow it up with plum pudding. I suppose it was because it was Christmas week. Comrade Bobok fell foul of the mustard almost at once and only quenched himself by lengthy potations which, however, were all to the good as they put him into a good temper.

"The whole thing might have been carried off perfectly well had it not been for this blasted moth which had been circling the Georgian candlesticks since the start of the dinner-party and which now elected to get burnt and crawl on to Polk-Mowbray's side-plate to die. Polk-Mowbray himself was undergoing the fearful strain of decoding Comrade Bobok's weighty pleasantries which were full of corrupt groups and he let his attention wander for one fatal second.

"As he talked he absently groped in his side-plate for a piece of bread. He rolls bread balls incessantly at dinner, as you know. Spalding and I saw in a flash of horror something happen for which our long diplomatic training had not prepared us. Mind you, I saw a journalist eat a wine-glass once, and once in Prague I saw a Hindu diplomat's wife drain a glass of vodka under the impression that it was water. She let out a moan which still rings in my ears. But never in all my long service have I seen an Ambassador eat a moth—and this is precisely what Polk-Mowbray did. He has a large and serviceable mouth and into it Spalding and I saw the moth disappear. There was a breathless pause during which our poor Ambassador suddenly realized that something was wrong; his whole frame stiffened with a dreadful premonition. His large and expressive eye became round and glassy with horror.

"This incident unluckily coincided with two others; the first was that Drage walked on with a blazing pudding stuck with holly. Our guests were somewhat startled by this apparition, and Comrade Bobok, under the vague impression that the blazing pud must be ushering in a spell of diplomatic toasts, rose to his feet and cried loudly: 'To Comrade Tito and the Communist People's Serbian Trade and Timber Guild. *Jiveo!*' His fellow Serbs rose as one man and shouted: '*Jiveo!*'

"By this time, however, light had begun to dawn on Polk-Mowbray. He let out a hoarse jarring cry full of despair and charred moth, stood up, threw up his arms and groped his way to the carafe on the sideboard, shaken by a paroxysm of coughing. Spalding and I rocked, I am sorry to say, with hysterical giggles, followed him to pat him on the back. To the startled eyes of the Yugoslavs we must have presented the picture of three diplomats laughing ourselves to death and slapping each other on the back at the sideboard, and utterly ignoring the sacred toast. Worse still, before any of us could

turn and explain the situation Spalding's elbow connected with Drage's spinal cord. The butler missed his footing and scattered the pudding like an incendiary bomb all over the table and ourselves. The Yugoslav delegation sat there with little odd bits of pudding blazing in their laps or on their waistcoats, utterly incapable of constructive thought. Spalding, I am sorry to say, was racked with guffaws now which were infectious to a degree. De Mandeville who was holding the leg of the table and who had witnessed the tragedy also started to laugh in a shrill feminine register.

"I must say Polk-Mowbray rallied gamely. He took an enormous gulp of wine from the carafe and led us all back to table with apologies and excuses which sounded, I must say, pretty thin. What Communist could believe a capitalist hyena when he says that he has swallowed a moth? Drage was flashing about snuffing out pieces of pudding.

"We made some attempt to save the evening, but in vain. The awful thing was that whenever Spalding caught De Mandeville's eye they both subsided into helpless laughter. The Yugoslavs were in an Irremediable Huff and from then on they shut up like clams, and took their collective leave even before the coffee was served.

"It was quite clear that Spalding's Timber Pact was going to founder in mutual mistrust once more. The whole affair was summed up by the *Central Balkan Herald* in its inimitable style as follows: 'We gather that the British Embassy organized a special dinner at which the Niece de Resistance was Glum Pudding and a thoroughly British evening was enjoyed by all.' You couldn't say fairer than that, could you?"

For Immediate Release

"Most F.O. types", said Antrobus, "are rather apt to imagine that their own special department is more difficult to run than any other; but I must say that I have always handed the palm to you Information boys. It seems to me that Press work has a higher Horror Potential than any other sort."

He is right, of course. Antrobus is always right, and even though I am no longer a foreign service type I am proud to be awarded even this tardy recognition when all is said and done.

A press officer is like a man pegged out on an African ant-hill for the termites of the daily press to eat into at will. Nor are we ever decorated. You never read of a press officer getting the George Cross for rescuing a reporter who has fallen into his beer. Mostly we just sit around and look as if we were sickening for an O.B.E.

And what can compare with the task of making journalists feel that they are loved and wanted—without which they founder in the Oedipus Complex and start calling

41

for a Parliamentary Commission to examine the Information Services? Say what you like, it's an unenviable job.

Most of the press officers I've known have gradually gone off their heads. I'm thinking of Davis who was found gibbering on the Nan Tal Pagoda in Bangkok. All he could say was: "For Immediate Release, absolutely immediate release." Then there was Perry who used to boil eggs over a spirit-lamp in the office. He ended by giving a press conference in his pyjamas.

But I think the nicest and perhaps the briefest press officer I have ever known was Edgar Albert Ponting. He was quite unique. One wonders how he was recruited into so select a cadre. He was sent to me as second secretary in Belgrade. I had been pressing for help for some time with a task quite beyond me. The press corps numbered some fifty souls—if journalists can be said to have souls. I could not make them all feel loved and wanted at once. Trieste with its ghastly possibilities of a shooting war loomed over us: propaganda alone, I was told, could keep the balance—could keep it a shouting war. I turned to the Foreign Office for help. Help came, with all the traditional speed and efficiency. After two months my eleventh telegram struck a sympathetic chord somewhere and I received the information that Edgar Albert was on the way. It was a great relief. Fraternization with the press corps had by this time raised my alcohol consumption to thirty *slivovitza* a day. People said they could see a pulse beating on the top of my head. My Ambassador had taken to looking at me in a queer speculative way, with his head on one side. It was touch and go. But it was splendid to know that help was at hand. It is only forty odd hours from London to Belgrade. Ponting would soon be at my elbow, mechanically raising and lowering his own with the old Fleet Street rhythm press officers learn so easily.

Mentally, I toasted Ponting in a glass of sparkling Alka Seltzer and called for the *Immediate* file. From Paris came the news that he had not been found on the train. After a wait of four days a signal came through saying that he had been found. He was at present in St. Anne's due for release later in the day when his journey would be resumed. I was rather uneasy as I remembered that St. Anne's was a mental hospital, but my fears subsided as I followed his route and saw him safely flagged into Switzerland and down into Italy. There was an ominous pause at Pisa which lasted ten days. Then came a signal from the Embassy in Rome saying that our vice-consul there had located him and put him on the train. This was followed by an odd sort of telegram from Ponting himself which said: *"Can't tell you what impression Leaning Tower made on me old man. On my way. Avanti. Ponty."*

At Venice there was another hold-up, but it was brief. Our vice-consul was away. It appeared that Ponting had borrowed 1,000 lire from the consulate gondolier and represented himself to the clerks in the consulate as a distressed British subject domiciled in Lisbon. All this was of course disquieting, but, as I say, one gets used to a highly developed sense of theatre in press officers. They live such drab lives. Once he was through Trieste and Zagreb, however, I began to breathe more freely, and make arrangements to meet him myself.

The Orient Express gets in at night. I had planned a quiet little dinner at the flat during which I would unburden myself to Ponting and brief him as to the difficulties which faced us. (A visit from the Foreign Minister impended: rumours of Russian troop movements were at meridian: trade negotiations with Britain were at a delicate phase: and so on and so forth.)

He was not at the station: my heart sank. But Babic, the Embassy chauffeur, interrogated the wagon-lit attendant, and we learned with relief that Ponting had indeed arrived. "He must have walked," said the attendant, "he had very little luggage besides the banjo. A little case like a lady's handbag."

We drove thoughtfully up the ill-paved streets of the capital and down Knez Mihailova to the only hotel set aside for foreign visitors (all the others had been turned into soup-kitchens and communal eating-houses). He was not at the hotel. I was standing at the desk, deep in thought, when the circular swing-doors of the hotel began to revolve, at first with slowness, then with an ever-increasing velocity which drew the eyes of the staff towards them. Somebody not too certain of his bearings was trying to get into the hotel. It seemed to me that he was rather over-playing his hand. By now the doors were going round so fast that one thought they would gradually zoom up through the ceiling, drawn by centrifugal force. Ponting was inside, trapped like a fly in amber. I caught sight of his pale self-deprecating face as he rotated grimly. It was set in an expression of forlorn desperation. How had this all come about? Could he have mistaken these massive mahogany doors for a bead curtain? Impossible to say. He was still holding his banjo to his bosom as he swept round and round. There was an impressive humming noise as of a nuclear reactor reacting, or of a giant top at full spin. Ponting looked dazed but determined, like a spinster trapped in a wind-tunnel. A small crowd of servants formed at a respectful distance to observe this phenomenon. Then without warning the second secretary was catapulted out of the swing-doors into our midst, like someone being fired out of a gun into a net. We recoiled with him, falling all over the staircase. For a brief moment his face expressed all the terror of a paralytic whose wheel chair has run away with him and is heading straight for the canal. Then he relaxed and allowed himself to be dusted down, gazing anxiously at his banjo all the time. "Thank God, Ponting, at last you're here," I said. I don't know why I should take the name of God in vain at a time like this; the words just slipped out.

He introduced himself in rather a mincing fashion. His eyes were certainly glassy. I put him down as a rather introverted type. I must say, however, that his opening remark "could not but" (as we say in despatches) fill me with misgiving. "This '*slivovitza*'," he said hoarsely, "it's a damn powerful thing. I'm practically clairvoyant, old man. You mustn't be shirty with old Ponting." He wagged a finger forlornly, helplessly. He looked as if he too needed to feel loved and wanted.

Physically he was on the small side, pigeon-chested and with longish arms which ended in fingers stained bright yellow with nicotine. He had the mournful innocent eyes of a mongrel. "Ponting," I said, "you'd better have a little rest before dinner." He did not protest, but leaning heavily against me in the lift he said under his breath, but with conviction: "If ever I get the Nobel Prize it won't be for nuclear physics." In my heart of hearts I could not help agreeing with him.

He laid himself out on his bed, kicked off his shoes, folded his arms behind his head, closed his eyes and said (in the veritable accents of Charlie McCarthy): "Quack. Quack. Quack. This is Ponting calling." Then in a different voice: "Did you say Ponting? Surely not Ponting."

Then reverting again to the dummy he so much resembled: "Yes Ponting. *The* Ponting, Ponting of Pontefract."

"Ponting," I said severely.

"Quack Quack," responded the dummy.

"Ponting, I'm going," I said.

He opened his eyes and stared wildly round him for a moment. "Is it true that the Ambassador lives on nightingale sandwiches?" he asked. There were tears in his eyes. "The *Daily Express* says so." I gave him a glance of cold dignity.

"I shall speak to you tomorrow," I said, "when you are sober." I meant it to sting.

By eleven o'clock next morning Ponting had not appeared and I sent the office car for him. He was looking vague and rather scared and had a large woollen muffler round his throat. His eyes looked as if they were on the point of dissolving, like coloured sweets. "Old man," he said hoarsely, "was there something you wanted?"

"I wanted to take you to H.E., but I can't take you looking like an old-clothes-man." He gazed down at himself in wonder. "What's wrong with me?" he said. "I bet you haven't got a shirt on under that scarf." I had already caught a glimpse of a pyjama jacket. "Well, anyway," said Ponting, "I can sign the book, can't I?"

I led him shambling through the Chancery to the Residence which I knew would be deserted at this hour. He made one or two hypnotist's passes at the Visitors' Book with streaming pen and finally delivered himself of a blob the size of a lemon. "It was the altitude," he explained. "My pen exploded in my pocket." I was busy mopping the ink with my handkerchief. "But you came by train," I said, with considerable exasperation, "not by air." Ponting nodded. "I mean the altitude of the Leaning Tower of Pisa," he said severely.

I led him back to the Chancery door. "Can I go back?" he asked humbly. "It takes a few days to acclimatize in a new post; H.E. won't be shirty with old Ponting, will he?"

"Go," I said, pointing a finger at the iron gates of the Embassy, "and don't come back until you are ready to do your job properly."

"Don't be shirty, old boy," he said reproachfully. "Ponting will see you through."

"Go," I said.

"In my last post," said Ponting in a brooding hollow sort of way, "they said I was afflicted with dumb insolence."

He traipsed down the drive to the waiting car, shaking his head sadly.

I was contorted with a hideous sense of desolation. What was to be done with a ventriloquist who played the banjo and spent half his time talking like a duck?

I went into the Chancery and took down the F.O. List to examine Ponting's background. His foreground had become only too apparent by now. He had had a number of posts, none of which he had held for more than a month or so; he had been moved round the world at breakneck speed, presumably leaving behind him in each town the indelible scars of a conduct which could only be excused by reference to the severest form of personality disorder. "Bitter fruit," I said to Potts the archivist. "Look at this character's record." He put on his spectacles and took the book from me. "Yes," he said. "In every post it would seem to be a case of retired hit-wicket. Poor Ponting!"

"Poor Ponting!" I said angrily. "Poor me!"

After that I did not see Ponting for several weeks. Once, late at night, my Head of Chancery surprised him in the lounge of his hotel doing a soft shoe routine and playing the banjo to a deeply attentive audience of partly sentient journalists. The heavy smell of plum brandy was in the air. In those days it cost about fourpence a glass. Ponting did a little song, a pitiful little spastic shuffle, and brought the performance to an end by pulling out his bow tie to the distance of a yard before letting it slap back on to his dicky. Antrobus, then first secretary, witnessed all this with speechless wonder. "By God," he said fervently, "never have I seen an Embassy let down like this. He popped his cheek at me in a dashed familiar fashion and said he had once acted in a pierrot troupe on Clacton pier. I couldn't bring him to his senses. He was . . ." words failed him. He reported the matter to H.E. who, from the armoury of his diplomatic experience, produced the word which had eluded Antrobus. "Bizarre," he said gravely. "I gather this fellow Ponting is a little bizarre."

"Yes, sir," I said.

"It's awfully peculiar," he said. "Your predecessor was an Oxford Grouper. He was bizarre too. At press conferences he would jump up and testify to the most awful sins. Finally the press protested." He paused. "If you don't mind my saying so," he said, "a large proportion of the Information Section in the F.O. seems a bit . . . well, bizarre." I could see that he was wondering rather anxiously what my particular form of mental trouble might be.

"I'm afraid Ponting will have to go."

"Well, if you say so. But as he's been civil enough to

sign the book I must give him a meal before he leaves."

"It would be unwise, sir."

"Nevertheless I will, poor fellow. You never know what he has on his mind."

"Very good, sir."

From then on Ponting became a sort of legendary figure. I tried to find him from time to time but he never seemed to be in. Once he phoned me to say that he was taking up a lot of contacts he had made and that I was not to worry about him. He had made a hit with the press, he added, everybody loved old Ponting and wanted him. I was so speechless with annoyance I forgot to tell him that telegrams suggesting his recall had already been sent to the Foreign Office. One day Antrobus came to my office; he appeared to be within an ace of having a severe internal haemorrhage. "This man Ponting", he exploded, "must be got out of the country. Britain's good name. . . ." He became absolutely incoherent.

"What's he done now?" I asked. Antrobus for once was not very articulate. He had met Ponting, dressed as a Roman centurion, walking down the main street of the town at twelve noon that morning. He had been, it seemed, to a fancy dress ball given by the Yugoslav ballet and was on his way back to his hotel. "He was reeling," said Antrobus, "absolutely reeling and speechless. Rubber lips, you know. Couldn't articulate. And the bastard popped his cheek at me again. And gave me a wink. Such a wink." He shuddered at the memory. "And that's not all," said Antrobus, his voice becoming shriller. "That's by no means all. He rang Eliot at three o'clock in the morning and said that H.E. didn't understand the Trieste problem and that he, Ponting, was going to open unilateral negotiations with Tito in his own name. I gather he was prevented by the tommy gunners on Tito's front door from actually carrying out his threat. Mark me, we shall hear more of this." Ponting's future never looked darker. That afternoon we got a call from the Ministry of Foreign Affairs. They wished to deliver an *aide mémoire* to the Embassy. Montacute went. He was the new Counsellor. He came back an hour later mopping his brow. "They say Ponting is a Secret Service agent. Unless we withdraw him he'll be declared *persona non grata*." I gave a sigh of relief. "Good. This will force the F.O.'s hand. I'll get off an Immediate." I did. The answer came back loud and clear that evening: "*Edgar Albert Ponting posted to Helsinki to leave by earliest available means.*"

Armed with this telegram I set out to find him. He was not at the hotel, nor at the only two restaurants available for foreigners. He was not at the Press Club though Garrick of the *Mirror*, who was expiating his sense of frustration in triple *slivovitzas*, told me he'd seen him. "He was trapped in the lift some hours ago. Dunno where he went afterwards." I finally ran him to earth in a Balkan *bistro* with an unpronounceable name. He was sitting at the bar with a girl on each side. His face was lifted to the ceiling and he was singing in a small bronchial voice:

> *I'm the last one left on the corner,*
> *There wasn't a girl for me,*
> *The one I loved married anovver,*
> *Yes anovver, yes anovver,*
> *Oo took 'er far over the sea.*

He was so moved by his own performance that he began to cry now, huge round almost solid tears which rained down and marked the dusty bar. This sort of behaviour is fairly normal among Serbs whenever they are drunk and the tragedy of The Great Panslav idea comes to mind. The girls patted him sympathetically on the back. "Poor old Ponty," said Ponting in hollow self-commiserating tones. "Nobody understands Ponty. Never felt loved and wanted." He blew his nose insanely in a dirty handkerchief and drained his glass. This cheered him. He said in a good strong cockney voice:

> *Come fill me with the old familiar jewce*
> *Mefinks I shall feel better bye and bye . . .*

"Ponting," I said. "There's some news for you."

He took the telegram in shaking fingers and read it out slowly like a peasant reading the Creed. "What's it mean?" he said.

"You're off tomorrow. There's a crisis in Helsinki which brooks of no delay. Ponting, the F.O. have chosen *you*. Your country is calling."

"Ta ra ra ra," he said irreverently and stood to the salute. We were all irresistibly impelled to do the same, the Serbian girls, the bartender and myself. It was the last memory I was to carry away of Ponting. I have often thought of him, and always with affection and respect. Some years ago I saw that he had transferred to the Colonial Office, and from that day forward, believe it or not, you could hardly open a newspaper without reading about a crisis in the colony where Ponting happened to be posted. Maybe it's only the sheer momentum of Ponting's influence which is pushing the Empire downhill at such a speed. I shouldn't be at all surprised.

White Man's Milk

"The Grape," said Antrobus with a magisterial air as he stared into the yellow heart of his Tio Pepe, "the Grape is a Rum Thing. I should say it was the Diplomat's Cross —just as I should say that in diplomacy a steady hand is an indispensable prerequisite to doing a job well. . . . Eh? The tragedies I've seen, old boy; you'd never credit them."

"Ponting?"

"Well, yes—but I wasn't even thinking of the element of Human Weakness. But just think of the varieties of alcoholic experience which are presented to one in the Foreign Service. To take one single example—National Days."

"My God, yes."

"To drink vodka with Russians, champagne with the French, *slivovitz* with Serbs, *saki* with Japs, whisky and Coca Cola with the Yanks . . . the list seems endless. I've seen many an Iron Constitution founder under the strain. Some get pooped by one drink more than another. There was a Vice-Consul called Pelmet in Riga. . . ."

"Horace Pelmet?"

"Yes."

"But he didn't drink much, did he?"

"No. But there was one drink which he couldn't take at all. Schnapps. Unluckily he was posted to Riga and then Oslo. At first he was all right. He used to get slightly dappled, that was all. Then he started to get progressively pooped. Finally he became downright marinated. Always crashing his car or trying to climb the sentries outside the Embassy. We managed to hush things up as best we could and he might have held out until he got a transfer to a wine-growing post. But what finished him was a ghastly habit of ending every sentence with a shout whenever he was three or four schnapps down wind. You'd be at a perfectly serious reception exchanging Views with Colleagues when all of a sudden he'd start. You'd hear him say—he started quite low in the scale—"As far as I, Pelmet, am concerned"—and then suddenly ending in a bellow: "British policy IS A BLOODY CONUNDRUM." I heard him do this fourteen times in one evening. The German Minister protested. Of course, poor Pelmet had to go. They held him *en disponibilité* for a year or so but no Chief of Mission would touch him. He died of a broken heart I believe. Took to wood-alcohol on a big scale. Poor fellow! Poor fellow!"

He sighed, drained his glass and raised a long finger in the direction of the bar for reinforcements. Merlin the steward replenished the glasses silently and withdrew.

"But the unluckiest chap of all", continued Antrobus after a short pause, "was undoubtedly Kawaguchi, the Jap Minister in Prague. His downfall was Quite Unforeseen. Poor chap."

"Tell me about him."

"His was a mission of some delicacy. He started off frightfully well. Indeed, they were an enchanting couple, the Kawaguchis. They spoke nothing but Jap, of course, which sounds like someone sand-papering a cheese-wire. With the rest of the Corps they were silent. Both were tiny and pretty as squirrels. Their features looked as if they had been painted on to papier mâché with a fine brush. At functions they sat together, side by side, holding on to their own wrists and saying nothing. But they were full of the small conventional diplomatic politeness —always sending round presents of sweets or paper fans with 'Made in Hong Kong' printed on them. Once I saw her laugh—she made a funny clicking sound. As for him, I don't honestly know how he conducted his business with the Czechs. There was some sort of trade pact being discussed at the time. Perhaps he used telepathy. Or perhaps he'd discovered some sort of Central European tic-tac. His whole mission consisted of two typist-clerks and a butler, none of whom spoke Czech. Anyway the important thing is this: the Kawaguchis never drank anything but *saki* which they imported in little white stone bottles. As you know it's a sort of brew from millet or something. . . ."

"Salty and mildly emetic."

"Yes: well, when they had to go out to a banquet or rout he always sent his butler over in the afternoon with a few small bottles of the stuff which were always placed before him at table. It was a familiar sight to see the two of them sitting there with their *saki* bottles before them. And so it was on this fatal evening which I am about to describe to you. It was New Year's Eve, I think: yes, and the French had elected to give a party. They always did things better than anyone else. The Kawaguchis were there, sitting in a corner, looking about them with their usual air of dazed benevolence. It was late and the party was in full swing. The usual petty scandals had enjoyed their usual public manifestation—the wife of the Finnish Consul had gone home in a huff because her husband had disappeared into the garden with the wife of the French First Secretary. A Russian diplomat was being sick in the Gentlemen's cloakroom. A nameless military attaché was behaving foully . . . we won't go into that. The general nostalgia had afflicted the band and a whole set of Old Viennese Waltzes was being played non-stop. As you know, it is a jolly difficult dance and can verge on the lethal. I always take cover when I hear 'The Blue Danube' coming up, old man."

"So do I."

"Well, imagine my astonishment when I saw the Kawaguchis rise from their chairs. They had never been known to dance, and at first I thought they were leaving. But something curious in their attitude drew my attention. They were gazing at the dancers like leopards. They both looked dazed and concentrated—as if they had been attending an ether party. Then he suddenly seized her round the waist and they began to dance, to the astonishment and delight of everyone. And they danced perfectly—a real Viennese waltz, old man, impeccable. I felt like cheering.

"They went round the floor once and then twice: everything under control. Then, old man, a ghastly premonition of the worst came over me, I can't tell why. Was it an optical illusion or were they dancing a bar or two faster than the music? I waited in an agony of impatience for them to come round again. It was only too true. They were one bar, two bars out of time. But their spin was absolute perfection still. By now, of course, the

band began to feel the squeeze and increased the time. Indeed, the whole thing speeded up. But as fast as they overtook the Kawaguchis the faster did the two little Japs revolve. Perhaps in some weird Outer Mongolian way they thought it was all a race. I don't know. But I, who know the dangers and pitfalls of the Old Viennese Waltz, felt my throat contract with sympathy for them. There was no way one could help. A terrible blackness of soul came over me—for all his Czech colleagues were there on the floor dancing with their wives. It could only be a matter of time now. . . . The speed had increased to something like the Farnborough Air Show. Lots of people had dropped out but the floor was still quite full. The Kawaguchis were still travelling a dozen light-years ahead of the band, and the band with popping eyes was pumping and throbbing at its instruments in an attempt to catch them up. But by now they were no longer a dancing couple. They were a Lethal Weapon."

Antrobus paused and lit a cigarette with a shaking hand. Then he went on sadly. "The first to go was the Czech Minister of Finance, with whom Kawaguchi had been doing so frightfully well in negotiation. There was a sudden sharp crack and the next moment he was sitting on a violinist's knee holding his ankle while his wife stood ineffectually beating the air for a moment before subsiding on top of him. The Kawaguchis noticed nothing. They were in a trance. On they went. A series of collisions, trifling in themselves, now began to take place. The Chief Economic Adviser to the Treasury, Comrade Cicic, was dancing with a wife whose massive proportions and enormous buffer constituted a dance floor hazard at the best of times. In a waltz it was hair-raising to image what might happen.

"I calculated that if the Kawaguchis struck her they would certainly be halted dead. Not a bit of it. This frail little couple had achieved such a terrific momentum that when they struck Mrs. Cicic there was a dull crash only: a powder-compact in her evening bag exploded causing a cloud of apparent smoke to rise. When it cleared Mrs. and Mr. Cicic were reeling into the corner while the Kawaguchis were speeding triumphantly on their way. They had entered into the spirit of the waltz so deeply now that they were dancing with their eyes closed. There was something Inscrutably Oriental about the whole thing. I don't remember ever being so excited in my life. I began to tick off the casualties on my fingers. By now there were quite a number of walking-wounded and one or two near-stretcher cases; everywhere one could hear the astonished whispers of the Corps: 'C'est Kawaguchi qui l'a fait. . . .' 'Das ist Kawaguchi. . . .' But on they went, scattering destruction, and perhaps they would be going on still had not someone deflected them.

"I still don't quite remember how. All I remember is that all of a sudden they were off the floor and moving through the tables and chairs with the remorselessness of a snow-plough. At the end of the ballroom there were some tall french windows which were open. They opened on to a long terrace at the end of which there was an ornamental lake in the most tasteless post-Versailles tradition. Nevertheless. The Kawaguchis vanished through the french windows like a meteor, and such was the dramatic effect they had created that everyone rushed out after them just to see what would happen, including the band which was somehow still playing. It was just as if someone at a children's party had shouted: 'Come and look at the fireworks.' We all poured out on the terrace shouting and gesticulating. The Spanish Ambassador was shouting: 'For God's sake stop them. STOP THEM. Caramba!' But there wasn't any stopping them.

"The tragic but unbelievably beautiful momentum of their waltz had carried them into the shallow lake. Normally it would be snowbound but Prague had had a thaw this year. They sat, utterly exhausted but somehow triumphant in a foot of water and stench, smiling up at their colleagues of the Corps. The cold night air and the water which enveloped them seemed to be having a calming effect, but they made no effort to get out of the pond. They just stared and smiled quaintly. It was only then that I realized they were both drunk, old man. Absolutely pooped. People had come with lights now, and Czech doctors and alienists had appeared from everywhere. There were even some members of the Czech Red Cross with blankets and stretchers.

"We waded into the swamp to recover our colleague and his wife and after a bit of argument emptied them both into stretchers. I shall never forget her smile of sheer beatitude. Kawaguchi's face expressed only a Great Peace. As they bore him off I heard him say, more to himself than anyone: 'Oriental man different from White Man.' I have always remembered and treasured that remark, old boy. Something like the same thing was said by the French chargé's wife: 'How your Keepling say: "Ist is Ist and Vest is Vest"?' But I was sorry for the Kawaguchis. Magnificent as the whole thing was, here we were, with three minutes to go before midnight, simply covered in mud and confusion. Some of the women had tried to draw attention to themselves by rushing into the swamp after them. The Italian Ambassador had a sort of Plimsoll line in the middle of his dress trousers. The ballroom looked like an advance dressing-station on the Somme. It is impossible to pretend that the evening wasn't ruined. And above all, the dreadful smell. Apparently all the drains flowed into this romantic little lake. It was all very well so long as it wasn't disturbed. The French were definitely confused, and I for one was sorry for them. No Mission could carry off a thing like this lightly."

Antrobus blew out his cheeks and lay back in his arm-chair, keeping a watchful eye on me to see that I had fully appreciated all the points in the drama. Then he went on in his usual churchwarden's style: "The Kawaguchis left for Tokyo by air the next afternoon. His mission was a failure and he knew it. I must say that there were only two Colleagues at the airport to see him off—myself and the perfectly foul military attaché about whom I will never be persuaded to speak. He was deeply moved that we had troubled to find out the time of his departure from the Protocol. I wrung his hand. I knew he wasn't to blame for the whole thing. I knew it was purely Inadvertent."

"How do you mean?"

"The butler gave the whole thing away some weeks later. Apparently the normal case of *saki* had not come in that month. They were out of drink. There was nothing a responsible butler of any nationality could do. He took some of the *saki* bottles and filled them with . . . guess what?"

"Bad Scotch whisky."

"Dead right! 'White Man's Milk' he called it."

"Awfully bad luck."

"Of course. But we face these hazards in the Foreign Service, don't we?"

"Of course we do."

"And we outlive them. Kawaguchi is in Washington."

"Bravo! I'm so glad."

"Care for another whiff of Grape-Shot before we lunch?"

Drage's Divine Discontent

"Did I ever tell you about the time when Drage, the Embassy butler, began to suffer from visions? No? Well, it was dashed awkward for all concerned and Polk-Mowbray was almost forced to Take Steps at the end.

"You probably remember Drage quite well: a strange, craggy Welsh Baptist with long curving arms as hairy as a Black Widow. A moody sort of chap. He had a strange way of gnashing his dentures when he spoke on religious matters until flecks of foam appeared at the corners of his mouth. For many years he had been a fairly devout fellow and always took a prominent part in things like servants' prayers. He also played the harmonium by ear at the English church—a performance to be carefully avoided on Sundays. For the rest one always found him hunched over a penny Bible in the buttery when he should have been cleaning the M. of W. silver. His lips moved and he made a deep purring sound in his throat as he read. We were all, frankly, rather scared of Drage.

"The awful thing about him was that he wore a wig

63

so obvious that he gave one the impression of having just stepped off the stage after a successful performance as Caliban. It was an indeterminate badger-grey affair which left a startling pink line across his forehead. The gum-like colour of the integument simply didn't match the rocky blueish skin of his face. Everyone knew it was a wig. Nobody ever dared to say so or allude to it.

"As for the visions, he confessed later that they had been gaining on him for some considerable time, and if he never mentioned them before it was because he felt that once we all recognized him as the Lord's Anointed we might give him the sack, or at least ask him to step down in favour of Bertram the footman. As you see, there were flashes of reason in the man. But all this intense Bible-squeezing could not help but have an effect on him, and one night at a party given for the Dutch Ambassador he dropped his tray and pointed with shaking finger at the wall behind Polk-Mowbray's head, crying in the parched voice of an early desert father: 'Here they come, sor, in all their glory! Just behind you, sor, Elijah up, as sure as I'm standing here!' He then covered his eyes as if blinded by the vision and fell mumbling to his knees.

"While in one sense one felt privileged to be present at Drage's Ascension into Heaven by fiery chariot, nevertheless his timing seemed inconsiderate. First of all poor Polk-Mowbray sprang to his feet and overturned his chair. Our guests were startled. Then to make things worse the Naval Attaché who dabbled in the occult and who hated to be left out of anything pretended to share Drage's vision. I think he had been drinking pink gins. He pointed his finger and echoed the butler. 'There they go!' he said in cavernous tones. 'Behind you!'

" 'What the deuce is it?' said Polk-Mowbray nervously, seating himself once more, but gingerly.

"Benbow slowly moved his pointing finger as he traced the course of the Heavenly Host round the dining-room table. 'So clear I can actually touch them,' he said. He was now pointing at De Mandeville who had changed colour. He leaned forward and touched the Third Secretary's ear-lobe. De Mandeville gave a squeak.

"As you can imagine the whole atmosphere of our dinner party was subtly strained after this. Bertram led Drage off into the wings in a rather jumbled state and bathed his brow from a champagne bucket. Benbow was sent to Coventry by common consent. Nevertheless, he spent the rest of the evening in high good humour, occasionally pointing his finger and saying indistinctly: 'Here they come again.' He kept the Dutch looking over their shoulders.

"Naturally, one could not tolerate visions during meals and when Drage recovered Polk-Mowbray told him to cut it out or leave. The poor butler was deeply troubled. Apparently he had discovered that he had never been baptized and this was preying on his mind. 'Well,' said Polk-Mowbray, 'if you think baptism will cure you of visions I can easily arrange with Bishop Toft to give you a sprinkle. He arrives next week.'

"Twice a year the Bishop of Malta came in for a couple of days to marry, baptize or excommunicate the members of the Embassy living in exile amidst the pagan Yugoslavs. He was, as you remember, a genial and worldly bishop, but hopelessly absent-minded. He brought in with him a sort of acolyte called Wagstaffe who was spotty and adenoidal and did the washing-up of thuribles or whatever acolytes have to do. He was simply Not There as far as the Things Of This World are concerned. He was a Harrovian. It stuck out a mile. Well, this year the bishop's visit coincided with that of Brigadier Dilke-Parrot. In fact they came in the same car and stood being noisily genial in the hall as their bags were unstrapped. The brigadier, who was large and red and had moustaches like antlers, also came every year on some mysterious mission which enabled him to have two days' shooting on the snipe-marshes outside the town. He always brought what he was pleased to call his '*Bundook*' with him—a twelve-bore by Purdy. This year there appeared to be two gun-cases—pay attention to this—and the second one belonged to the bishop. It contained a magnificent episcopal crook, taller when all the bits were screwed together than the bishop himself. These two very similar cases lay side by side in the hall. Thereby hangs my tale.

"Drage greeted Bishop Toft with loud cries of delight and weird moppings and mowings and tugs at his forelock. He explained his case and the bishop rather thoughtfully agreed to baptize him. But here there was an unexpected hitch: Drage refused to be baptized in his wig; he wanted to feel the Jordan actually flowing on his cranium, so it was agreed that the baptism should take place in the privacy of the buttery where the butler could reveal all. A drill was worked out. After the ceremony Drage would replace his foliage and the bishop would then walk ahead of him, holding his crook, to the ballroom where the rest of the Embassy staff would be waiting to receive his ministrations. There were half a dozen babies to baptize that year.

"Well, Drage knelt down, and there was a tearing noise like old canvas. A large polished expanse of dome was presented to the bishop. He said afterwards that he blenched rather because Drage looked so extraordinary. Bits of dry glue were sticking to his scalp here and there. Well, the Bishop of Malta was just about to read the good news and anoint the butler when Wagstaffe opened the leather case and found that it contained the brigadier's '*bundook*'. It was imperative to acquaint the bishop with this mishap as he could hardly walk into the crowded Embassy ballroom holding a shotgun like a hillbilly. But how to interrupt Toft who by now was in mid-peroration? Wagstaffe had always been an irresolute person. He could hardly call out: 'Hey, look at this for an episcopal crook.' He fitted the barrel and stock together with the vague idea of holding it up for the bishop to see. He did not look to see if it was loaded. He started working his way stealthily round the kneeling Drage to where he might catch the bishop's eye.

"But it was the eye of the butler which first lighted on the weapon. He had always been a suspicious person and now it seemed as clear as daylight that while the bishop was holding him in thrall Wagstaffe had orders to stalk him from behind and murder him. Perhaps the shot would be a signal for the massacre of Baptists everywhere. Drage's Welsh heritage came to the surface multiplying his suspicions. And to think that this silver-haired old cleric went about getting Baptists murdered. . . . A hoarse cry escaped his lips.

"The irresolute acolyte started guiltily, and as Drage scrambled to his feet, he dropped the gun on to the carpet where it went off. The brigadier had always boasted of its hair-trigger action.

"The dull boom in the buttery sounded frightfully loud to the rest of us in the ballroom across the corridor.

It was followed by a spell of inarticulate shouting and then all of a sudden Drage appeared, running backwards fairly fast, pursued by the bishop with his sprinkler, making vaguely reassuring gestures and noises. Wagstaffe staggered to the door deathly pale and fainted across the two front rows of as yet unbaptized babes. They set up a dreadful concert of frightened screams.

"It was a dreadful scene as you can imagine. Drage disappeared into the garden and was only persuaded to come back and finish his baptism by the united efforts of Benbow, De Mandeville and myself. Moreover, he felt humiliated to be seen wigless by the whole Embassy. It took some time to straighten things out, specially as the mud-stained brigadier had by now arrived in a fearful temper, holding the episcopal crook between finger and thumb with an expression of the deepest distaste on his face.

"But as it happens things turned out very well. A pair of bright brown eyes had observed the downfall of Drage. To Smilija, the second housemaid, Drage's baldness seemed a wonderful thing. She had never realized how beautiful he could be until she saw his cranium taking the sunlight. It was a revelation and love now entered where formerly indifference only was. . . . They are married now; the visions have stopped; his wig has been sold as a prop to the Opera Company. You occasionally see it in the chorus of *Parsifal*. Which illustrates another little contention of mine: namely that Everybody Is Somebody's Cup Of Tea. Another one before we dine?"

"Noblesse Oblige"

"The case of Aubrey de Mandeville is rather an odd one. I often wonder what the poor fellow is doing now. He wasn't cut out for Diplomacy—indeed it puzzles me to think how Personnel Branch could have considered him in any way the answer to a maiden's prayer at all. It was all due to Polk-Mowbray's folly, really."

"I don't remember him."

"It was the year before you came."

"Polk-Mowbray was Ambassador?"

"Yes. He'd just got his K.C.M.G. and was feeling extremely pleased about it. He'd invited his niece Angela to spend the summer at the Embassy and it was I think this factor which preyed on his mind. This Angela was rather a wild young creature—and as you know there was not much to do in Communist Yugoslavia in those days. I think he rather feared that she would fall in with a hard-drinking Serbian set and set the Danube on fire. His dearest wish was that she should marry into the Diplomatic, so he hit upon a brilliant scheme. He would order someone suitable through Personnel and do a bit of match-making. Scott-Peverel the Third Secretary was married. He would have him replaced by Angela's hypothetical Intended. A dangerous game, what? I warned him when I saw the letter. He wanted, he said, a Third Secretary, Eton and Caius, aged 25 (approx.), of breeding and some personal fortune, who could play the flute. (At this time he was mad about an Embassy Quartet which met every week to fiddle and scrape in the Residence.) He must have known that you can't always depend on Personnel. However, despite my admonitions he sent the letter off and put the wheels in motion for Bunty Scott-Peverel's transfer to Tokyo. That was how we got De Mandeville. On paper he seemed to fill the bill adequately, and when his Curriculum Vitae came Polk-Mowbray was rather disposed to crow over me. But I kept my own counsel. I had Doubts, old boy, Grave Doubts.

"They were unshaken even by his personal appearance ten days later, sitting bolt upright in the back of a Phantom Rolls with the De Mandeville arms stencilled on the doors. He was smoking a cheroot and reading the Racing Calendar with close attention. His chauffeur was unloosing a cataract of white pig-skin suitcases, each with a gold monogram on it. It was quite clear that he was a *parvenu*, old boy. Moreover the two contending odours he gave off were ill-matched—namely gin-fumes and violet-scented hair lotion of obviously Italian origin. He condescendingly waved a ringed hand at me as I introduced myself. It had been, he said, a nerve-racking journey. The Yugoslavs had been so rude at the border that poor Dennis had cried and stamped his foot. Dennis was the chauffeur. 'Come over, darling, and be introduced to the Man,' he cried. The chauffeur was called Dennis Purfitt-

Purfitt. You can imagine my feelings, old man. I felt a pang for poor Polk-Mowbray and not less for Angela who was lying upstairs in the Blue Bedroom sleeping off a hangover. 'Dennis is my pianist as well as my chauffeur,' said De Mandeville as he dismounted holding what looked like a case of duelling pistols but which later turned out to be his gold-chased flute.

"I must confess that I was a bit gravelled for conversational matter with De Mandeville. 'I'll take you to meet H.E. at eleven,' I said huskily, 'if you would like time for a rest and a wash. You will be staying a night or two in the Residence until your flat is ready.'

" 'Anything you say, darling boy,' he responded, obviously determined to be as agreeable as he knew how. In my mind's eye I could see Angela weeping hot salt tears into her pillow after her first meeting with De Mandeville. It was just another of Personnel's stately little miscalculations. However, I held my peace and duly presented him all round. His interview with Polk-Mowbray lasted about fifteen seconds. Then my telephone rang: Polk-Mowbray sounded incoherent. It is clear that he had received a Mortal Blow. 'This ghastly fellow,' he spluttered. I tried to soothe him. 'And above all,' said Polk-Mowbray, 'impress on him that no Ambassador can tolerate being addressed as "darling boy" by his Third Secretary.' I told De Mandeville this with a good deal of force. He curled his lip sadly and picked his nose. 'Now you've hurt little Aubrey,' he said reproachfully. 'However,' and he drew himself together adding: 'Little Aubrey mustn't pout.' You can imagine, old boy, how I felt.

"De Mandeville's job as Third Secretary was largely social, looking after appointments and visitors and arranging *placements*. I could not help trembling for Polk-Mowbray. The new Third Secretary would sit there at his desk taking snuff out of a gold-chased snuff-box and reading despatches through a huge magnifying glass. He was a *numéro* all right.

"His first act was to paint his flat peacock blue and light it with Chinese lanterns. He and the chauffeur used to sit about in Russian shirts under a sun-lamp playing nap or manicuring their nails. Angela went steadily into a decline. Once when he was an hour late for dinner at the Embassy he excused himself by saying that he had gone upstairs to change his rings and had been simply unable to decide which to wear. He used to have his hair waved and set every month, and made the mistake of going to a Serbian hairdresser to have it done. You know how game the Serbs are, old man? Terribly willing. Will always do their best. They waved De Mandeville's hair into the crispest bunch of curls you are ever likely to see outside Cruft's. It was ghastly. Polk-Mowbray was almost beside himself. He wrote a long offensive letter to Personnel accusing them of sending out a steady stream of female impersonators to foreign posts and smirching the British name, etc.

"De Mandeville himself seemed impervious to criticism. He just pouted. So long as he confined his social activities to his own sphere he was not dangerous. But as time went on he found the diplomatic round rather boring and decided to take the Embassy in hand. His *placements* became more vivid. He also began a series of ill-judged experiments with the Residency Menus. Some of the more nauseating local edibles found their way on to the Embassy sideboards under stupefying French names. I remember a dinner at which those disgusting Dalmatian

sea slugs were served, labelled '*Slugs Japonaises au Gratin*'.
The naval attaché went down after this meal with a pro-
longed nervous gastritis. A Stop Had To Be Put to De
Mandeville; of course by now Polk-Mowbray was working night and day to have him replaced—but these things
take time.

"Meanwhile the Third Secretary swam in the diplomatic pool in a hair net, took a couple of Siamese kittens
for walks with him on a lead, and smoked cigarettes in a
holder so long that it was always catching in things.

"His final feat of *placement*—he was dealing with central
European Politburo members of equal rank—was to have
the Embassy dining-table cut in half and a half-moon
scooped out of each end. When it was fitted together
again there was a hole in the middle for H.E. to sit in
while his guests sat round the outer circle. Polk-Mowbray was furious. He suffers terribly from claustrophobia
and to be hemmed in by this unbroken circle of ape-like
faces was almost more than flesh and blood could stand.

"On another occasion De Mandeville dressed all the
waiters in Roman togas with laurel wreaths: this was to
honour the twenty-first birthday of the Italian Ambassador's daughter. On the stroke of midnight he arranged
for a flock of white doves to be released—he had hidden
them behind screens. Well, this would have been all right
except for one Unforeseen Contingency. The doves flew
up as arranged and we were all admiration at the spectacle.
But the poor creatures took fright at the lights and the
clapping and their stomachs went out of order. They flew
dispiritedly round and round the room involuntarily be-
stowing the Order of the Drain Second Class on us all.
You can imagine the scene. It took ages to shoo them
through the french windows into the garden. The Roman

waiters had to come on with bowls and sponges and re-
move the rather unorthodox decorations we all appeared
to be wearing.

"But the absolute *comble* was when, without warning
anyone, he announced that there would be a short
cabaret to amuse the Corps at a reception in honour of
Sir Claud Huft, the then Minister of State. The cabaret
consisted of De Mandeville and his chauffeur dressed as
Snow Maidens. They performed a curious and in some
ways rather spirited dance ending in an abandoned *can-
can*. It was met with wild applause: but not from Polk-
Mowbray as you can imagine. He found the whole
episode Distasteful and Unacceptable. De Mandeville
left us complete with pigskin suitcases, flute-case, and
chauffeur in the Great Rolls. We were all quite dry-eyed
at the leave-taking. But it seemed to me then that there
was a Moral to be drawn from it all. Never trust Personnel Branch, old man.

"As for poor Angela she was in sad case. Polk-
Mowbray sent her to Rome for the Horse Show and—
guess what? She up and married a groom. It was a sort
of involuntary rebound in a way. Everyone was spell-
bound with shame. But she had the good sense to go off
to Australia with him, where I gather that one needs little
Protective Colouring, and there they are to this day. The
whole thing, old man, only goes to show that You Can't
Be Too Careful."

9

Call of the Sea

"I have never really respected Service Attachés," said Antrobus. "Some I have known have bordered on the Unspeakable—like that ghastly Trevor Pope-Pope. I don't know how he got into the Blues, nor why he was ever posted to us. He used to lock himself into the cipher-room and play roulette all day with the clerks. Skinned them all, right and left. He had no mercy on anyone. He also used to sell bonded champagne by the case to disagreeable Latin-American Colleagues for pesos. And to cap it all the fellow wore embroidered bedsocks.

"But as for 'Butch' Benbow, he was one of the least objectionable service postings. He was naval attaché, you remember."

"Yes."

"The fact that he was so decent makes the whole episode inexplicable. I really cannot decide in my own mind whether he did sever that tow-rope or not. And yet I saw him with my own eyes. So did Spalding. Yet the whole thing seems out of keeping with Benbow. But who

77

knows what obscure promptings may stir the heart of a
naval attaché condemned to isolation in Belgrade, hundreds of dusty miles from the sound of the sea? And then,
imagine being designated to a country with almost no
recognizable fleet. There was nothing for him to do once
he had counted the two ex-Japanese condemned destroyers
and the three tugs which made up Yugoslavia's quota of
naval strength. Nor can the horse-drawn barges on the
two dirty rivers, the Sava and the Danube, have had
much appeal. They filled him no doubt with a deep cor-
roding nostalgia for the open sea and The Men Who Go
Down To It In Ships. This might explain the sudden
brainstorm which overpowered him when he saw the
entire Diplomatic Corps afloat on the Sava. Human
motives are dark and obscure. I find it hard in my heart
to judge Benbow."

"When was all this?"

"The year after you were posted."

Antrobus waved his cigar and settled himself more
deeply in his favourite arm-chair. "It was a slack period
diplomatically and as always happens during slack periods
the Corps busied itself in trying to see which Mission
could give the most original parties. The Americans gave
an ill-judged moonlight bathing party on the island of
Spam during which the Corps swam as one man into a
field of jellyfish and a special plane had to be chartered to
bring medical supplies to those who were stung. Then
the Italians, not to be outdone, gave a party in a ruined
monastery surrounded with cherry orchards—a picturesque enough choice of *venue*. But the season was well
advanced and they had entirely failed to take into account
the Greater Panslav Mosquito—an entomological curiosity to be reckoned with. It is the only animal I know

which can bite effortlessly through trousers and under-pants all in one flowing movement. We all came back to Belgrade terribly swollen up and all different shapes and sizes. Then the Finns gave a concert of Serbian folk-music to which the band turned up drunk. Finally it seemed to Polk-Mowbray that it was our turn to be crea-tive and a chit was passed down asking for ideas.

"I think it was De Mandeville who suggested a river party. Certainly it was not Benbow's idea; he had been very subdued that winter and apart from confessing that he was clairvoyant at parties and dabbling in astrology he had lived an exemplary life of restraint.

"Nor, on the face of it, was the idea a bad one. All winter long the logs come down the River Sava until the frost locks them in; with the spring thaw the east bank of the river has a pontoon of tree-trunks some forty feet wide lining the bank under the willows so that you can walk out over the river, avoiding the muddy margins, and swim in the deep water. The logs themselves are lightly tacked together with stapled wire by the lumber-jacks and they stay there till the autumn when they are untacked again and given a push into mid-stream. They then float on down to the sawmills. Here, as you know, the diplomatic corps swims all summer long. Though the muddy banks of the stream are infested with mosquitoes the light river wind ten yards from the shore creates a free zone. And jolly pleasant it is, as you probably remember.

"Well, this was the site selected for a river party by candle-light—the summer nights are breathlessly still—and Polk-Mowbray threw himself into the arrangements with great abandon. First of all he made sure that over the selected area the logs were really tacked firmly together. An immense tarpaulin was then spread and nailed down.

This made a raft about a hundred feet by sixty—big enough even to dance on. The Sava water cushioned the thing perfectly. A light marquee was run up and a long series of trestles to take a buffet. It promised to be the most original party of the year—and I'm not sure in retrospect whether it wasn't the most original I have ever attended. De Mandeville and his chauffeur were in the seventh heaven of delight; they organized a wickerwork fence round the raft with little gates leading to the dance floor and so on. There was also a changing-room for those who might decide to stay on and bathe. All in all it was most creditable to those concerned.

"The Corps itself was in ecstasies as it climbed the brightly painted gangplank on to the raft with its gaily lit buffet and striped marquee. Everyone turned up in full splendour and Polk-Mowbray himself made what he called his Special Effort: the cuff-links given to him by King Paul of Greece, the studs given to him by Queen Marie of Rumania, the cigarette-case by De Gaulle, and the cigar-cutter by Churchill. Darkness and candlelight and the buzz of Diplomatic Corps exchanging Views were offset by the soft strains of Bozo's Gypsy Quartet which played sagging Serbian melodies full of glissandos and vibratos and long slimy arpeggios. It was an enchanting scene. The Press Corps was represented by poor Tope (Neuter's Special Correspondent) who was rapidly transported into nirvana by the awfully good Bollinger.

"You will ask yourself how the thing could possibly have gone wrong—and I cannot answer you for certain. All I know is that out of the corner of my eye I think I caught sight of a figure—was it Benbow?—sneaking furtively among the willows on the bank with what seemed to be a hatchet in his hand. More I cannot say.

"But I can be definite about one thing; while everyone was dancing the rumba and while the buffet was plying a heavy trade, it was noticed that the distance between the raft and the shore had sensibly increased. The gangplank subsided in the ooze. It was not a great distance— perhaps ten feet. But owing to the solid resistance such a large raft set up in the main current the pull was definitely outward. But as yet nobody was alarmed; indeed most of the members of the Corps thought it was part of a planned entertainment. I suppose most of the passengers on the *Titanic* turned in the night before the iceberg with just the same comfortable sense of well-being.

"Polk-Mowbray himself was concerned, it is true, though he did not lose composure. 'Can't some of you secretaries get out and push it back to the bank?' he asked; but the water was already too deep. For a long minute the lighted raft hung like a water-fly on the smooth surface of the river and then slowly began to move downstream in the calm night air, the candles fluttering softly, the band playing, and the Corps dancing or smoking or gossiping, thoroughly at peace with itself. There was at this stage some hope that at the next bend of the river the whole thing would run aground on the bank, and a few of us made preparations to grab hold of the log pontoons or the overhanging willows and halt our progress. But by ill luck an eddy carried us just too far into the centre of the river and we were carried past the spit of land, vainly groping at the tips of bushes.

"By now our situation deserved serious thought. There was literally no stop now until we reached Belgrade and here—the sweat started out on me as I thought of it—the Danube joins the Sava and causes something like a tidal

bore, a permanent whirlpool. While the Sava is comparatively sluggish the Danube comes down from Rumania at
about fourteen knots—impossible to swim in or ford.
The point of junction is just below the fortress of
Belgrade, a picturesque enough spot for those on dry
land. . . .

"It was about five minutes before the full significance
of our position began to dawn upon the Corps and by this
time we were moving in stately fashion down the centre
of the fairway, all lit up like a Christmas tree. Expostula-
tions, suggestions, counter-suggestions poured from the
lips of the diplomats and their wives in a dozen tongues.

"Unknown to us, too, other factors were being introduced which were to make this a memorable night for us
all. Yugoslavia, as you know, was hemmed in at this time
by extremely angry Communist states which kept her in
a perpetual state of alarm by moving troops about on her
borders, or by floating recriminatory and sometimes por-
nographic literature down the rivers which intersected
the country—in an attempt, one imagines, to unman
Serbian Womanhood, if such a thing be possible. At any
rate, spy-mania was at meridian and the Yugoslav forces
lived in a permanent state of alertness. There were fre-
quent rumours of armed incursions from Hungary and
Czechoslovakia. . . .

"It was in this context that some wretched Serbian
infantryman at an observation post along the river saw
what he took to be a large armed man-of-war full of
Czech paratroops in dinner jackets and ball-dresses sailing
upon Belgrade, the capital. He did not wait to verify this
first impression. Glaucous-eyed, he galloped into Belgrade castle a quarter of an hour later on a foam-flecked
mule with the news that the city was about to be invested.

The tocsin was sounded, while we, blissfully unaware of this, sailed softly down the dark water to our doom.

"It was lucky that there was only one gun in Belgrade castle. This was manned by Comrade Popovic and a scratch team of Albanian Shiptars clad in skull caps of white wool and goatskin breeches. (Fearsome to look at because of his huge moustache and shapeless physique the Shiptar is really a peaceable animal, about as quarrelsome as a Labrador and with the personality of a goldfish.) Usually it took the team about a week to load the Gun, which was a relic left behind them by the departing Visigoths or Ostrogoths—I forget which. Strictly speaking, too, it was not an offensive weapon as such but a Saluting Gun. Every evening during Ramadan it would give a hoarse boom at sunset, while a pair of blue underpants, which had been used from time immemorial as wadding for the blank charge, would stiffen themselves out on the sky.

"Nevertheless, when the news of the invasion reached Comrade Popovic he realized in a flash that the defence of the city depended entirely on him. He closed his eyes for a brief moment and saw himself receiving, in rapid succession, the Order of the Sava, The Order of St. Michael First Class, the Order of Mercy and Plenty with crossed Haystacks, and the Titotalitarian Medal of Honour with froggings. He set his platoon the task of scraping together a lethal charge capable of scattering the invaders as they came round the bend in the river. This was to be composed of a heterogeneous collection of beer bottle tops, discarded trouser buttons, cigarette-tins and fragments of discarded railway train. The aged gun was slewed round after a violent spell of man-hauling and brought to bear upon the target area.

"Meanwhile things aboard the raft were not going too well. Signs of incipient disintegration had begun to set in. Some of De Mandeville's artful trellis work had gone while the whole buffet had rather surprisingly broken off from the main body and started on a journey of its own down a narrow tributary of the river. I still remember the frozen faces of the waiters as they gazed around them despairingly like penguins on an ice-floe. Bozo's Band still kept up a pitiful simulacrum of sound but they had to keep moving position as the water was leaking along the tarpaulin and enveloping their ankles. Many of the candles had gone out. The chill of despair had begun to settle on the faces of the diplomats as the full urgency of the situation became plain to them. In their mind's eye they could hear—not to mix a metaphor—the fateful roar of the Danube water in its collision with the slow and peaceful Sava. Involuntary exclamations burst from the more voluble ladies. Was there nothing we could do? Could we not signal? Perhaps if we lit a fire . . . ? But these were counsels of despair as well they knew. I think we all felt in our bones that we should have to swim for it. The Italian Ambassador who had not swum for a quarter of a century tried a few tentative strokes in the air in a vain attempt to remember the routine. The only lucky person was Tope who had fallen asleep under the bar and was being borne off steadily down the tributary towards the sawmills where presumably he would be cut up by absent-minded Serbs and turned into newsprint— a fitting end.

"By this time we had reached the fatal bend in the river overlooked by the bastions of the castle where Pithecanthropos Popovic waited, eyes on the river, safety match at the ready. The Gun was loaded to the brim. He knew he could not afford to miss us as it would be at least a week before the raw material for another lethal charge could be gathered from the dustbins of Belgrade. It was now or never. He drew a deep ecstatic breath as he saw us come round the bend, slowly, fatefully, straight into his line of fire. He applied the safety match to the touch-hole.

"There was a husky roar and the night above us was torn by a lurid yellow flash while the still water round the raft was suddenly ripped and pock-marked by a hail of what seemed to us pretty sizeable chain-shot. Pandemonium broke out. 'My God,' cried the Argentine Minister, who always showed a larger White Feather than anyone else, 'they're shooting at us!' He took refuge behind the massive Hanoverian frame of Madame Hess, wife of the German First Secretary. 'Throw yourselves on your faces!' cried the Swiss Minister, suiting the action to the word. The Italian Ambassador refused this injunction with some hauteur. 'Porca Madonna, I shall die standing up,' he cried, striking an attitude with one hand on his breast.

"Though nobody was actually hurt the bombardment had carried away most of the band's instruments, half the marquee and the rest of the De Mandeville's dainty trellis-work. It had also holed an ice-box filled with tomato juice and scattered the stuff, with its fearful resemblance to blood, all over us, so that many of us looked cut to pieces. Nor did we know then that it would take Comrade Popovic a week to repeat his exploit. We expected a dozen more guns to open on us as we neared the city. Some of the ladies began to cry, and others to staunch the apparent wounds made by the flying tomato juice on their menfolk. The Argentine Minister, suddenly noticing a red stain spreading on his white dinner-jacket front cried out: 'Caramba! They've got me!' and fell in a dead faint at Madame Hess's feet.

"The raft looked like a Victorian battle-piece by a master of anecdote. Some lay on their faces, some crouched behind chairs, some stood gesticulating, but all were racked with moans. It was now, too, that Polk-Mowbray turned savagely on poor De Mandeville and hissed: 'Why don't you do something? Why don't you shout for help?' Obediently above the racket De Mandeville raised his pitiful female-impersonator's screams: 'Help! Help!' into the enigmatic night.

"No further guns barked at us from the fort but by now the river had narrowed and its flow had increased. The raft began to spin round and round in a series of sickening rotations as it neared the fateful junction. Ahead of us we could see the blaze of searchlights and the stir of river traffic. My God, what fresh trials were awaiting us down there at the whirlpool's edge? Perhaps squads of whiskered Serbs were waiting to greet us with a hail of small-arms fire. A green-and-red rocket shot up in the farther darkness, increasing our alarm.

"Now the only people who had been of any real assistance to us in our predicament (though we did not know it then) were the chauffeurs of the Diplomatic Corps. They were mostly Serbian and virtually constituted a Corps on their own; jutting foreheads, lowering forelocks, buck teeth, webbed hands and feet, vast outcrops of untamed hair stretching away to every skyline. . . . They alone had watched our departure with alarm—with shrill ululations and inarticulate cries as they shifted their feet about in the ooze and watched the raft borne to its destruction. Moreover, they remembered what happened at the confluence of the two rivers. No sooner, therefore,

were we out of sight than the chauffeurs started out for town—a long gleaming line of official limousines.

"They had the sense, moreover, to go down to the dock and alert the river police and to enlist the aid of all the inhabitants of the coal quay whose bum-boats might be of use in grounding the raft before it reached the Niagara Falls. Two police boats with searchlights and a variety of sweat-stained small-boat owners accordingly set off up the Sava to head us off. This was the meaning of the lights and rockets on the river which caused us so much alarm.

"But they had reckoned without the mean size of the raft; even with all the missing bits which had flaked off it was still the size of a ballroom floor and correspondingly heavy. The bum-boats and the river launches met us in sickening collision about four hundred yards above the river junction. We were by this time so confused and shaken as to be almost out of our minds. Most of us thought that we had been attacked by pirates, and this impression was heightened when a huge Serb picked up Madame Hess in one hand and deposited her in his bum-boat. Cries of 'Rape!' went up from the Latin-American secretaries who had seen this sort of thing before. Meanwhile, half-blinded by searchlights and repeatedly knocked off their feet by the concussion of launches hitting the raft, the Swedish Embassy, in one of those sudden attacks of hysteria which afflict Nordics, decided to die to the last man rather than allow our rescuers aboard. The friendly, willing Serbs suddenly found themselves grappled by lithe young men clad in dinner jackets who sank their teeth into their necks and rolled overboard with them. A disgraceful *fracas* ensued. Despite the powerful engines of the river launches, too, the raft was irresistibly moving towards the rapids carrying not only the Flower of European Diplomacy but also a large assortment of bum-boats whose owners were letting out shrill cries and rowing in every direction but the right one.

"It was all over with us, old man. Not exactly in a flash but in a series of movements like a bucking bronco. Those of us who had read Conrad's *Typhoon* felt we had been here before.

"The Danube ripped the tarpaulin off, unstapled the logs and threw everything into the air. It was lucky that there were enough logs to go round. I can't say the Diplomatic Corps looked its best sitting astride logs with the water foaming round it, but it was certainly something you don't see every day. The Argentine Minister was borne screaming off into the night and only picked up next morning ten miles down river. Indeed, the banks of the Danube as far as the town of Smog were littered with the whitening bones of Swedes and Finns and Japs and Greeks. De Mandeville was struck on the head and knocked insensible; Polk-Mowbray broke his collar bone. Draper lost a toupee which cost about a hundred pounds and was forced to go about in a beret for nearly two months.

"We could not call the roll for twenty-four hours and when we did it seemed nothing less than a miracle that we had endured no major casualties. It's the sort of thing which almost makes one Take Refuge in Religion.

"As for Benbow, he had gone on long leave by next morning and was not due back for six months. It was a tactful retreat. Polk-Mowbray himself drew the moral and adorned the tale by remarking to the Chancery: 'The Great Thing in Diplomacy is Never to Over-reach Oneself.' I think he had got hold of something there, even if he was just being wise after the event."